UNIPIGGLE
The Unicorn Pig!

She's a muddy princess

He's a muddy unicorn pig

Together, they're a PERFECT match!

Keep your eyes peeled for
the little spider sneaking
through this book...

To Juno and Merry, who will work magic
on whatever they put their minds to.

First published in the UK in 2021 by Usborne Publishing Ltd., Usborne House,
83-85 Saffron Hill, London EC1N 8RT, England, usborne.com

Usborne Verlag, Usborne Publishing Ltd., Prüfeninger Str. 20,
93049 Regensburg, Deutschland VK Nr. 17560

Text and illustrations copyright © Hannah Shaw, 2021

A CIP catalogue record for this book is available from the British Library.

ISBN 9781474991148   07149/1   JFMAM JASOND/21

Printed in UAE.

MIX
Paper from
responsible sources
FSC® C004800

UNIPIGGLE
~ The Unicorn Pig! ~

Witch
Emergency

HANNAH SHAW

USBORNE

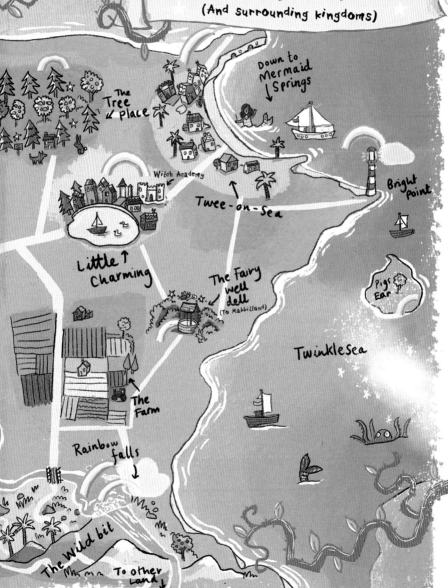

WELCOME TO

This is Princess Peony Peachykins Primrose Pollyanna Posh, usually known as Princess Pea. She lives in Twinkleland Palace with her parents, Queen Bee and King Barry.

She likes: mud, marshmallows, chocolate and having fun.

TWINKLELAND!

This is Unipiggle. He's Princess Pea's Royal Companion. He's a loud, muddy and proud unicorn pig.

He likes: mud, marshmallows, chocolate, having fun and getting tickled behind the ears.

Princess Pea was supposed to choose a **UNICORN** as her Royal Companion. But during the Unicorn Parade, there was a **STORM** and things went a bit **WRONG**. Luckily, Unipiggle saved the Princess and the day.

Now Princess Pea and Unipiggle are the best of friends and they love to have adventures together!

It was lucky the princess didn't choose a real unicorn because they refuse to get their hooves muddy!

A Secret Spell Book

It was a shiny Twinkleland morning and
Unipiggle and Princess Pea had just been to
Twinkletown Library. Unipiggle loved the library
because of the snuggly beanbags he could nap
on. Princess Pea loved the
library because
there were
so many
interesting
books.

Her Perfect Princess Schedule was full of lessons and chores, so it wasn't easy to have the sort of muddy, outdoor adventures she loved, but the Princess could always find time for a reading adventure!

"Trot a little faster, Unipiggle!" Princess Pea urged her podgy piggy friend, as they started up the steep hill that led to Twinkleland Palace.

Unipiggle broke into a canter and Princess Pea held on tight to his rainbow horn. He grunted happily as they passed under the giant marshmallow tree, then skidded to a stop at the glittering palace gates.

"Good day, Princess and Unipiggle!" The Gate Pixie smiled and unlocked the gates with his big gold key. "You look very cheerful this morning."

"*Cheerful! Cheerful!*" chorused the daisies that grew along the edge of the perfectly manicured palace gardens.

Cheerful!

Cheerful!

"Yes, we are!" replied Princess Pea, but she didn't say why. She thought it best that only she and Unipiggle knew about the magical library book she had hidden in her satchel...

Princess Pea had discovered the book by accident. She'd been giggling over a story about smelly fairies, when she'd noticed a strange glow radiating out from under a bookshelf. Filled with curiosity, she kneeled down on the floor and felt around under the shelf until her hand grasped what turned out to be a large and heavy book. With some difficulty, she pulled it out. The book must have been there for quite some time because it was very dusty. (Dust was rare in Twinkleland because dusting was such a popular hobby.)

Princess Pea wiped the dust off the cover to reveal a shimmering title: **Super Spells & Extra ordinary Enchantments.**

The book began to glow again. Princess Pea could feel it was positively **tingling** with magic and her heart skipped a beat.

"Wow, Unipiggle! Look at this!" she whispered.

15

Unipiggle rolled off his beanbag and oinked excitedly (but quietly — they were still in a library, after all).

The librarian wizard was fast asleep and snoring loudly. Princess Pea decided not to wake him, so she stamped the book herself and left him a note.

Dear Mr Wizard,
You were asleep when we borrowed a book:
Super Spells and Extraordinary Enchantments by Gurtrude Moon
Borrower: Princess Pea, Twinkleland Palace.

On the way home, Princess Pea had begun
to wonder whether the spell book should have
been in Twinkletown Library at all. Everyone
knew that **NO MAGIC** was
one of the many rules
of Twinkleland.

Important Rules

Be perfect

There must be no grubbiness

Be neatly completely

Politeness at all times

Check: are you smiling
cheerfully?

No laziness or dawdling

Do NOT use magic*

*except in a big and terrible
emergency

King
Barry   Queen Bee

Queen Bee liked to tell Princess Pea stories of messy **magical disasters**, such as the Strawberry Yoghurt Flood and the Never-Ending Firework Calamity, which had led to the rule in the first place. It was important to the Queen that the kingdom was kept immaculate and running like clockwork. The unicorns, fairies, pixies and dragons would never use magic on purpose. Even the friendly witches and wizards who lived in Little Charming weren't allowed to conjure things — they could only ride broomsticks and cook in cauldrons; spells were **strictly forbidden**.

Princess Pea didn't much like following the rules. She believed magic was fun, useful and… **delicious**. Unipiggle had his own special

(and secret) magic which meant he could turn
anything into chocolate! But what if they could
conjure up even more excitement?

Now they were back at the palace, Princess
Pea had a plan. "Would you like to learn some
new magic from the spell book, Unipiggle?" she
asked, tickling him behind the ears.

Unipiggle grunted eagerly — he was ready for
anything! It was time for a **MAGICAL**
adventure...

Pumpkin Disaster

Princess Pea and Unipiggle were desperate to try out some spells, but they couldn't risk getting caught.

"Let's head to our treehouse, Unipiggle!"

To start with, they needed to avoid Princess Pea's mummy. Queen Bee was out inspecting the First Best Garden with a feather duster and her Cobweb Removal Team — pixies who worked hard to keep the palace sparkling clean.

Princess Pea and Unipiggle hastily tiptoed over the glass bridge to the Second Best Garden. They passed King Barry riding on his golden tandem, his purple moustache billowing out behind him, and the Bicycle Pixie puffing with effort. Princess Pea waved at him while

Unipiggle quickly trotted towards the Third Best Garden. Hardly anyone from the palace bothered to visit this garden, but their friend Arthur the Gardener Pixie still kept everything perfectly pruned and sprouting splendidly.

NO SPLASHING IN THE POOL

SIT AND SMELL THE ROSES

After checking they were definitely alone, Princess Pea dismounted from Unipiggle and climbed through the gap in the hedge that led to the apple orchard and her secret treehouse. Princess Pea scrambled up her treehouse ladder while Unipiggle *boing*ed up using a carefully-placed giant marshmallow as a springboard.

BOING!

(He had tried and failed many times to climb
the ladder, and it just so happened that the
marshmallows that grew outside the palace
were super springy as well as yummy!)

The Princess's heart beat a little faster as she opened her satchel to lift out the magnificent, glowing spell book.

Unipiggle sniffed it curiously…

Achooo!

Together they turned to the first page. Princess Pea felt the tingle of magic once more as she began to read aloud:

Contents

 Reversal Spells

Not happy with your spell? Fear not, for a reversal spell will change things back to normal. IMPORTANT: Reversal spells must be performed by midnight on the day you cast the original spell. After midnight, all magic effects will become fully permanent.

"Ooh!" squeaked Princess Pea, flicking through the book. "There's so much choice, Unipiggle! Which spell first? Some of these sound rather complicated... But even if we go wrong, we've got plenty of time to try a reversal spell!"

Unipiggle frowned and grunted. Then he gently turned back to the second page with his snout.

Easy Vegetable-growing Spell:

Find a vegetable.
Use a wand, magical horn or enchanted baguette to point at the vegetable.
Chant "GROW-GROW-GROW" until your vegetable reaches the required size.
Clap three times to stop.

"You point and I'll chant, Unipiggle," decided the Princess. "Now, for the vegetables…?"

Unipiggle oinked and led Princess Pea out to where Arthur the Gardener Pixie had grown some lovely orange pumpkins.

Princess Pea smiled. "Great plan, Unipiggle. Arthur will be very pleased if his pumpkins are the biggest in Twinkleland!"

They chose three pumpkins. Unipiggle carefully aimed his horn at the first one…

ZAP!

They looked closer… But Princess Pea had
forgotten to chant! The pumpkin was the same
size, only now it was made from chocolate.

As Princess Pea munched on the delicious
chocolate pumpkin, Unipiggle tried again…

ZAP!

"Grow-grow-grow!" said Princess Pea firmly.

Another chocolate pumpkin!

This wasn't as easy as they'd thought.

With a very determined look, Unipiggle
aimed his horn squarely at the third pumpkin.

A rainbow of magic hit the pumpkin with some force. It glowed brightly…

The pumpkin shuddered...

...and juddered...

...and began to get **bigger!**

"It's working, Unipiggle!" the Princess cried.

Unipiggle did a little jump of joy as the pumpkin grew bigger than him.

Princess Pea thought that would be big enough, so she clapped her hands three times. But to her dismay, the pumpkin kept growing... and growing!

33

The Princess was clapping
with all her might while Unipiggle
stamped his trotters, but the
pumpkin was already as big as
Arthur's shed. It bulged
worryingly and its skin began to
stretch and creak.

"Yikes!" yelled Princess
Pea. "Take cover!"

36

The pumpkin exploded just as King Barry and the Bicycle Pixie pedalled around the corner. Their tandem's wheels skidded in the pumpkin goo and they toppled head first into the vegetable bed.

BOOM!
SPLAT!

Luckily, no one appeared to be hurt.

"Oops!" Princess Pea looked at Unipiggle. Unipiggle looked at Princess Pea. Then they picked up the now-very-sticky spell book…and ran all the way back to the treehouse to hide it.

"Barry? What was that noise?" The Queen dashed around the corner, followed by a group of concerned pixies.

King Barry huffed. He wasn't sure what had just happened, but he was covered in mud and orange goo was dripping off his crown.

Queen Bee spotted a trail of squelchy boot and trotter prints heading away across the grass.

"This comes as no surprise!" Queen Bee sighed as she helped the King and the poor pixie to their feet. "Our dear daughter and that

naughty pig of hers are causing trouble again.
I despair. When is she going to start acting
like a **Perfect Princess**?"

King Barry frowned. "Is my moustache
ruined?"

Just then, the Trumpet Pixie ran up to them, followed closely by the Announcement Pixie.

Tooty-tooty-parp-parp!

"Your Highnesses!" began the Announcement Pixie. Then she stopped and gaped at the King and the mess.

"Well, what is it?" asked the Queen.

A visitor! We have a visitor!

Uninvited Guests

The visitor stood in the Grand Hall, leaning on her shiny broomstick and looking around curiously. She was young and stylish, with blue hair and a sly smile. It was very rare to have an uninvited visitor at Twinkleland Palace, so the Queen was feeling flustered as the King slowly dripped pumpkin mush and mud onto the spotless marble floor beside her.

Princess Pea and Unipiggle were eavesdropping through an open window. They were curious to see who this visitor was, but, sensibly, they thought it best if they stayed out of sight for a while.

The King had pulled out his mirror to check his moustache and was absent-mindedly eating a little bit of pumpkin mash. "And what did you say your name was?"

"I'm Tallulah Twist from the town of Little Charming." The visitor smiled, revealing a set of perfectly pearly-white teeth. "I'm a *very experienced* **Prince and Princess Trainer**," she boasted.

"Really?" said the Queen in confusion. "Do all Princess Trainers have broomsticks, wands and pointy hats?"

"Oh, silly me, I'll explain!" Tallulah laughed. "I *used* to be a witch. I never used any magic, of course, and I *always* followed the RULES, but now I'm in the business of Prince and Princess Training."

The Queen seemed impressed. "Excellent. You couldn't have arrived at a better time! Can you work with *really* unruly princesses...and their unicorn pig companions?"

Princess Pea and Unipiggle looked at each other and rolled their eyes.

The King looked thoughtful. "You mean Peasprout, my darling? Doesn't she already have ballet, singing, art, music and many other princessy-type lessons?"

Princess Pea nodded at Unipiggle. They had so many lessons that they had to work *even harder* to find time to have adventures, climb trees and play in the mud like they wanted to.

"Our daughter just blew up a giant pumpkin," cried the Queen. "She needs someone to put her back on track!"

"I am a specialist in taming and training particularly **unruly** princesses," replied Tallulah Twist. She reached into a bag that was attached to the end of her very obedient broomstick and unrolled a scroll for the King and Queen to inspect. "As you can see, I have had a lot of experience."

"Recommended by the Duchess of OopsyWoopsyLand…" the King read.

"And you were hired by the Prince Regent of UpsideDownyLand. Where is that?" asked the Queen.

"Oh, far away." Tallulah smiled sweetly.

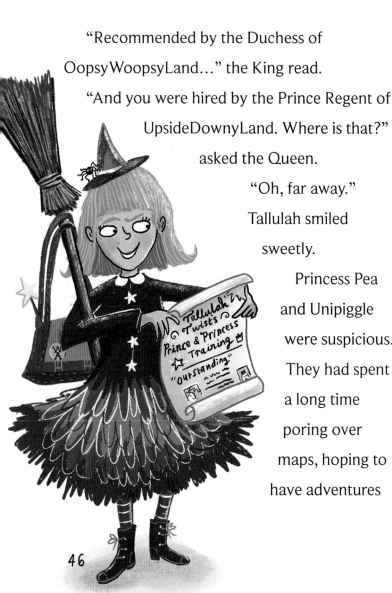

Princess Pea and Unipiggle were suspicious. They had spent a long time poring over maps, hoping to have adventures in far-away lands, and they hadn't heard of either of those places. "It sounds like she just made them up!" Princess Pea whispered.

"What do you want in return for your services?" Queen Bee asked Tallulah. "We will of course pay generously."

"Oh, I only ask for a comfortable room and meals for myself and Cedric," she replied. "And to read any books you might have…erm… hanging around in the palace."

"Who is Cedric?" enquired the Queen.

Tallulah Twist gave a little whistle and…

A huge, powerful white swan with the meanest little eyes waddled straight past them.

Hissss!

Unipiggle let out an oink of surprise.

Princess Pea decided it was time to put a stop to this nonsense. Neither she nor Unipiggle needed training. They knew exactly how to behave — they just didn't always want to!

Giving no time for the Announcement or Trumpet Pixies to introduce them, the Princess and Unipiggle stomped into the hall.

"Oh, Pea, darling! So glad you've come in," the Queen exclaimed. "Meet your new Princess Trainer, Tallulah Twist!"

"Delighted to meet you," said Tallulah, dropping the politest curtsey before turning to Unipiggle. "And you must be Unipiggle! I could smell you before I saw you," she said, with what seemed like a smirk.

Unipiggle looked at her proudly. He liked being pongy.

"You'll get on swimmingly with Cedric here. He just *loves* unicorns and…er…pigs, don't you, Cedric?"

Cedric narrowed his eyes.

"But, Mummy! Daddy! I don't need any more lessons!" protested Princess Pea crossly.

"I'm afraid we've made up our minds," said the Queen.

King Barry nodded, mainly because he was trying to dislodge a bit of pumpkin from his crown.

"Tallulah will have you polished up and behaving like a real princess in no time."

"Certainly," said Tallulah smoothly. "Now, would someone please show us our room? And do send up one of your sweet little pixies with some nibbles. I'm famished!"

Princess Pea and Unipiggle gaped as the pixies fussed around Tallulah like *she* was royalty.

"It's *very* strange she turned up out of nowhere like that," muttered Princess Pea to Unipiggle as they watched Tallulah sweep up the stairs. "I've never heard of a Princess Trainer before…"

Unipiggle frowned — he hadn't either.

"Cedric's not very friendly, is he?" the Princess continued. "We'll need to keep a really close eye on both of them. I don't trust them one little bit, Unipiggle. **Not one bit!**"

Princess Training

The next morning, Tallulah rudely strolled into Princess Pea's bedroom without so much as a knock on her door. Two anxious Wardrobe Pixies hurried in behind her, and one handed the sleepy Princess a schedule.

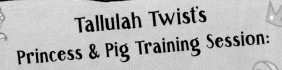

Tallulah Twist's
Princess & Pig Training Session:

Princess Makeover

-

Breakfast

-

Elegant Walking Lesson
Pig Dressage

-

Lunch

-

Sitting Still Lesson
Being Quiet Lesson

Unipiggle rolled out of bed and watched the Princess Trainer stride around the room.

"Where are your books? The only books I've found in this palace are pointless ones about cleaning, moustache styling and ukulele music. You should be reading books about princesses at the very least," Tallulah declared.

Princess Pea was about to tell Tallulah that she *did* read a lot, but she stopped herself, as her books were *definitely* not about being a princess. In fact, all of her books (including the new magical spell book) were in her treehouse and Tallulah Twist would *certainly* not be welcome there.

"You're a very scruffy princess. No wonder your parents needed to hire me!"

Tallulah laughed, now rifling through the
Princess's wardrobe.

Princess Pea shrugged, while Unipiggle
snorted at Tallulah's rudeness.

"Oh! What an adorable selection of dresses and shoes you have here!" Tallulah ordered the Wardrobe Pixies to bring Princess Pea a posh, puffy-skirted dress and a pair of pointy patent shoes that cramped her feet. "Go on then! Get changed!" she ordered bossily, waving her wand around.

Princess Pea didn't much like having a wand pointed at her, even if no one used them to do magic any more. She wondered why someone who *used* to be a witch would still keep one with her at all times.

Tallulah turned her attention to Unipiggle. "Bows. You need bows and ribbons and a huge lacy ruff!" she cackled.

Unipiggle tried to escape this torment by

hiding under the bed, but the pixies were so worried about pleasing Tallulah that they tickled him until he came out.

"Perfect!" declared Tallulah when the Wardrobe Pixies had finished with them both, although she looked more amused than pleased. "Now, off we go to show your parents."

Princess Pea and a disgusted Unipiggle clopped down to breakfast in their ridiculous outfits.

It seemed like the morning would never end as Princess Pea walked around the Second Best Lawn for the thirteenth time.

"Keep going! You need to improve your Perfect Princess posture!" Tallulah barked, while she lounged next to the pool, sipping a smoothie. Meanwhile, Unipiggle was having an equally miserable time doing dressage with

Cedric perched on his back. Unipiggle was actually quite good at posh trotting already, but today he was not at all happy, especially because he was wearing ridiculous ruffles and being sneakily pecked by a swan.

NO SPIDERS

"Is this all the reading matter you can find?"
Tallulah scolded a pixie who'd brought her a pile
of books from around the palace. She flicked
through them one by one, discarding them on
the ground.

It seemed very strange to Princess Pea that Tallulah seemed so interested in books, but didn't want to read any of them. She started to think of all the other things that made her suspicious about Tallulah: she had turned up unannounced, she had made up places that didn't exist and she was always pointing her wand. Not only that, but her lessons were more like Princess Torture than Princess Training! *What was she up to?* Princess Pea's feet ached in her silly shoes. She scowled at Tallulah as she stomped her way round the fourteenth lap of the lawn.

Finally, the bell rang for lunch and, without a word of praise, Tallulah immediately flew off on her broomstick. Princess Pea and Unipiggle took the opportunity to go and see their friend Arthur the Gardener Pixie (they still needed to apologize for exploding one of his pumpkins yesterday!).

Arthur opened his shed door and peered nervously out. "Are you sure you're alone? All the pixies in the palace are terrified of that swan and that bossy new teacher of yours. One of the Polishing Pixies told me she was made to spend the whole of last night searching the palace for something... A big dusty book that glows?"

Princess Pea and Unipiggle looked at him in astonishment.

"Sorry, Arthur, we've got to go. Quick, Unipiggle! To the treehouse! We can't let her find our book..."

Spells Disaster

The Princess and Unipiggle burst in through the treehouse door and rushed to open the suitcase where Princess Pea kept her books…

"Unipiggle! The spell book has gone!"

"Could this be what you're looking for?"
A smug voice came from behind them.

Princess Pea and Unipiggle spun round to see Tallulah Twist clutching **Super Spells and Extraordinary Enchantments**.

"Yikes!" Princess Pea yelled. "You really *were* after my book."

"I'll be confiscating this. Yuck, it's all covered

DINOSAURS

Magical Creature Guide

African

64

in pumpkin slime!" said Tallulah. "**No one**, especially not little princesses or silly **pigs**, should perform magic in Twinkleland…" She pointed her wand accusingly.

Unipiggle gave a worried squeal.

"But—" Princess Pea began.

"You don't want me to tell your parents that you had this book, do you now, Princess?" interrupted Tallulah. "I doubt they'd ever let you visit the library again…"

Princess Pea was fuming, but what could she do?

"Now for lunch!" Tallulah said breezily, clicking her fingers so her broomstick flew towards her over the orchard, doing some impressive loop-the-loops before hovering ready, at her side.

"You'll be pleased to know Cedric is in charge of your next training session, as I've got some reading to do. I hope you both enjoy sitting still…"

There was no way that Princess Pea and Unipiggle were going to sit still or be pecked at by a nasty swan while Tallulah Twist was up to no good. They snuck back into the palace.

Quickly, the Princess changed out of the puffy dress and into her cape, trousers and comfy wellies. Then she freed Unipiggle from his restrictive ruffle, feeling increasingly worried about Tallulah Twist's intentions. Why did she want that spell book? They *had* to find a way of getting it back…

The palace seemed eerily silent as they crept back down the spiral staircase. Usually there would be a Stair Pixie scrubbing the steps, or Cleaning Pixies mopping the corridors. The Princess couldn't even hear her daddy, the King, strumming his beloved ukulele.

Unipiggle leaped back. There was a frog inside the palace!

Princess Pea gently picked up the creature.

Down another flight of stairs, the Princess was astonished to find more frogs. Unipiggle grunted. It was very peculiar. The Palace Pixies would never normally allow garden creatures indoors.

Princess Pea took an ornamental urn from a table, scooped up the rest of frogs and carried them outside.

SNAP!

Yikes!

One of the daisies on the lawn was **snapping** at her ankles!

Grrrr!

The daisies were **growling**... Some had **TEETH!**

69

Unipiggle squealed and darted out of their way, but a rose bush reached out to grab his trotter, its thorny tendrils moving like an octopus's arms.

"The garden is attacking us!" cried Princess Pea, as another bush wrapped around her cape.

Unipiggle ducked as a crackle of sparks whooshed over his head. He oinked a warning to Princess Pea and together they took cover behind a statue, just as Tallulah Twist shot past on her broomstick.

Tallulah chanted and laughed as she pointed
her wand at things. *She* was the one turning the
plants into **vicious beasties**! This wasn't the fun
sort of magic Princess Pea had wanted to do. This
was terribly wrong and certainly *not* an exciting
adventure!

All of a sudden Cedric appeared, chasing the Trumpet Pixie along the path.

"**TOOOOOOT! TOOOOT!**" The Trumpet Pixie blew his horn in terror.

ZAAAAP!

Ribbit!

The Trumpet Pixie was now a frog!

Cedric hopped onto the back of Tallulah's broomstick and they whizzed away to enchant some sunflowers on the other side of the lawn.

"Nooo!" gasped Princess Pea.

Next to them,
a small shrub was
shaking. Princess
Pea could just
make out
a familiar face
behind the leaves.

Sob!

"Arthur?" asked
Princess Pea in alarm.
"Has Tallulah turned you into a tree?"

"No, it's just a disguise," Arthur squeaked
back. "That wicked swan tried to chase *me*
earlier so I quickly hid myself in these branches.
It appears I had a lucky escape!" He shuddered,
staring mournfully at the frog that used to be his
friend the Trumpet Pixie.

Princess Pea had a horrible realization. "Unipiggle, do you think those frogs we found were pixies too? We must tell my parents!"

Princess Pea and Unipiggle galloped back into the palace, followed by Arthur, who was too scared to take off his leafy camouflage. They burst into the Grand Hall…

Hopping all over the perfectly polished floor were more frogs, most of them wearing tiny pixie hats.

"Mummy! Daddy! You must come quickly," the Princess panted, glancing behind her to check Tallulah and Cedric hadn't seen them. "The Princess Trainer you hired is turning pixies into frogs and wreaking havoc in the garden. It's a **WITCH EMERGENCY!**"

Royally Enchanted

Princess Pea and Unipiggle stopped and blinked at the scene in front of them. Something was very wrong.

The two thrones in the Grand Hall were empty — the King and Queen had vanished! Instead, two unicorns were standing there…

One had a long purple mane and what looked like a moustache. It was chewing the stuffing out of a velvet sofa. The other was pink, wearing a small crown and nibbling on a lettuce leaf.

Neigh! Neigh!

"Uh oh, Unipiggle!" Princess Pea gulped. "Are those my parents?"

"Cantering carrots!" exclaimed Arthur-the-tree.

"Mummy Unicorn! Daddy Unicorn!" the Princess tried. "Tallulah Twist is using **MAGIC**! She's turned you into unicorns, the pixies into frogs…and the garden has gone completely **WILD**!"

The unicorns paused what they were doing and stared blankly at Princess Pea. Unipiggle oinked loudly and prodded the King Unicorn. The King Unicorn whinnied crossly and went back to eating the sofa.

"It's no use, Unipiggle. I don't think they understand." Princess Pea's eyes grew

wide as she remembered something else from the spell book. The spells would need to be reversed **before midnight** or they'd become permanent.

She checked the clock. It was already late in the afternoon.

The Princess took a deep breath. "Unipiggle, prepare yourself. We're going to have to try and stop Tallulah ourselves."

Unipiggle nodded seriously.

Princess Pea was just wondering exactly *how* they would stop Tallulah Twist, when...

Ding-a-ling!

Someone was ringing the entrance bell. Usually the Gate Pixie would open the gate for visitors, but Princess Pea looked out and couldn't spot him. Her heart sank as she realized

he may have met the same froggy fate as
the others.

"Come on, Unipiggle, let's see who it is before
Tallulah gets to them. Arthur, you can be the
lookout. Keep pretending to be a tree and warn us
if that tricksy Tallulah comes our way."

At the gate, the elderly wizard who worked in
the library was waiting impatiently.

"Ah, Princess Pea. Just the young lady I'm
looking for!"

The librarian wizard knew Princess Pea and
Unipiggle well because they were often in the
library and they seemed to bring **trouble**. There
had been a time when a huge dinosaur had

almost destroyed his library (and the whole of Twinkletown) while Princess Pea flew overhead on a dragon (but that's another story!).

Unipiggle picked up the key, which had been dropped on the path, and the Princess unlocked the gate.

"We need help, Mr Wizard. Hurry, there's no time to lose!" Princess Pea exclaimed. "And watch your step — the daisies bite!"

"I got your note…you know, the one about the…" The wizard stopped and did a nervous cough. "*Ahem*…about a certain book you borrowed yesterday. I need it back immediately! It shouldn't have been in the library at all."

"Sorry," said Princess Pea, urging him to keep walking. "I'm afraid we don't have it any more!"

"Oh, deary me, I'll be in so much trouble!" moaned the wizard. "A magic spell book certainly shouldn't have been in the library. The Queen ordered them all to be recycled into doormats years ago!" He paused again as they climbed the steps to the impressive front doors of the palace. "We don't want it to fall into the wrong hands… In fact, I knew I had to find you after I found your note, because I also got an urgent Twinklegram from the head teacher at the Little Charming Witch Academy. It informed me that a witch-in-training ran away yesterday… what was her name? Petula Mist or something? Apparently she is not to be trusted at all. She took her teacher's wand! Just think what someone like her might do with all those spells!"

"Could you mean Tallulah Twist?" asked Princess Pea. "I knew she wasn't really a Princess Trainer!"

Unipiggle shook his head in disbelief.

"Yes! That's her name — how did you know?"

Unipiggle gently nudged the wizard through the doors and into the Grand Hall.

"Your Highnesses!" gushed the librarian wizard as he bowed towards the thrones in the corner. Then he wiped his glasses. "Huh? Where did those unicorns come from?"

"They're my parents!" Princess Pea told him. "And I'm afraid you're too late. The spell book has already fallen into the wrong hands."

Princess Pea quickly told the wizard how
Tallulah had taken the spell book and was
casting terrible spells — including one which had
turned the King and Queen into unicorns. Worst
of all, they only had until **midnight** to stop her
or the spells would be everlasting!

"Jolly broomsticks!" cried the wizard,
mopping his brow.

Just then, Arthur
gave a shout.

> Hide, everyone!
> Tallulah and
> Cedric are
> headed this way!

Shrinking Wizard

Screeeeech!

Tallulah and her swan skidded to a halt at the doors to the palace and jumped off their broomstick. (It flew over to the umbrella stand and helpfully put itself away.)

Luckily, neither of them
spotted Princess Pea
and Unipiggle
crouched under the
dining table, the
librarian wizard
behind a curtain, or
Arthur disguised
as a tree outside.

Princess Pea took a
deep breath and willed
everyone to stay
quiet and still.
Tallulah sat on
the King's throne
and put her feet up.

Unipiggle frowned as he saw her take the crown from the Queen Unicorn to try on.

"What do you think, Cedric?" asked Tallulah. "Does it suit me?"

Cedric paused from chasing a terrified frog across the room and honked approvingly.

Tallulah opened the spell book. "Come on, King Unicorn! Let's make you jump!" She waved her wand around and chanted, "Clip-clop! Hippity-hop!"

The King Unicorn started jumping over the furniture and doing complicated posh trotting around the pixie-frogs while whinnying his head off. Princess Pea felt very sorry for her daddy, but Tallulah and Cedric seemed to think it was hilarious.

The librarian wizard couldn't contain his anger at such bad behaviour. He pulled back the curtain, brandishing his very rusty wand (which didn't work).

"That's enough!" he bellowed.

ZIP

ZAP

Yikes!

ZOOM

But before he could do anything else, Tallulah Twist had shrunk the librarian wizard.

"Oops! Did you come to get your book back? Now you're too small to even turn the pages!" Tallulah and Cedric snorted.

"Come on, Cedric." Tallulah continued with a smirk. "I want to keep playing Queen. Let's see if we can find a royal frock for me to wear!"

Princess Pea and Unipiggle were very relieved to see Tallulah and her swan prance upstairs.

"Are you okay, Mr Wizard…?"

The librarian wizard was speechless with rage.

At last he spoke in a teeny-weeny voice. "No one in Twinkleland is safe while that witch has that book! I need to fetch her head teacher Madame Merry from the Witch Academy in Little Charming – she'll be able to help." The Wizard scratched his head. *"The problem is, it's too far to walk and I left my broomstick at the library!"*

Unipiggle trotted over to the umbrella stand and tapped Tallulah's broomstick. It followed him obediently, waiting for a rider.

"Good thinking, Unipiggle. We'll send you on Tallulah's broomstick, Mr Wizard!"

"Oh, fiddlesticks… I'm too small to ride a broomstick!" complained the Wizard, looking down at his tiny feet.

Princess Pea and Unipiggle exchanged glances. Riding a broomstick sounded like a lot of fun, but they couldn't leave the palace with Tallulah on the loose. Who knew what further damage she might do while they were gone!

Arthur the Gardener Pixie shuffled forward, throwing off his branches. "I'll go!" he volunteered bravely. "And you can come with me, Mr Wizard."

After a few failed (and painful) attempts to stay on the broom, Arthur and the librarian wizard

(who was tucked safely into Princess Pea's old satchel) were finally in the air. It didn't really matter that Arthur was upside down. They were off!

"Good luck! Fly fast and bring help!" called Princess Pea.

Unipiggle oinked hopefully as he watched them disappear over the horizon.

"I hope they make it," Princess Pea whispered to her piggy companion. "In the meantime, we'll make it our mission to do all *we* can to **stop Tallulah**!"

Queen Witch

"More cake, Cedric?"

Tallulah had shut herself in the Queen's bedchamber.

"She's magicking up cupcakes and spilling cream and jam all over Mummy's Special Occasion Frock, but at least she's not turning pixies into frogs!" Princess Pea whispered to Unipiggle. She was standing on Unipiggle's back, spying on the devious duo through the keyhole. "Now Cedric is sitting on the spell book!"

Unipiggle snorted quietly with disgust.

Princess Pea climbed off his back and sighed.

She noticed that it was dark outside — time was ticking by and it would be **midnight** in just a few hours... She really hoped the librarian wizard and Arthur would return with Tallulah's head teacher soon, because she didn't fancy having unicorn parents for ever.

"Our only hope is to trap them both in there until help arrives. How can we do that, Unipiggle?"

Unipiggle's eyes lit up. He'd had an idea.

He tip-trotted off down to the garden and, before Princess Pea had even had time to worry, he had returned carrying Arthur's last pumpkin.

"Fantastic idea, Unipiggle! We'll block the door with a giant pumpkin. I'm sure we can do the vegetable-growing spell right this time."

Unipiggle aimed his horn and Princess Pea took a deep breath and muttered, "**Grow-grow-GROW!**"

The pumpkin swelled up until its stalk was touching the ceiling. Then Princess Pea clapped her hands very quietly three times…and…it stopped growing.

"Phew, Unipiggle! We did it!"

Unipiggled oinked… A little *too* loudly.

Oops.

"Did I hear that **PIG**, Cedric?" came Tallulah's voice from the Queen's bedroom. "I wondered where that Princess Pea and her pesky pet had got to!"

Princess Pea heard the door open.

-ZIP!- **-ZAP!-**

Princess Pea and Unipiggle were alarmed to see the pumpkin begin to shudder and shake.

"If I catch them, I'll turn them into scurrying mice!" Tallulah chortled.

BOOM!!

The pumpkin burst open.

Princess Pea and Unipiggle were splattered with goo.

And by the time they'd wiped it from their eyes...Tallulah and Cedric were standing menacingly in front of them!

Arthur to the Rescue

"Got you!" Tallulah raised her wand.

Princess Pea's wellies felt frozen to the spot!

Unipiggle squealed.

Zip…

At that very moment, Arthur flew in through an open window on Tallulah's broomstick.

He zoomed in front of Princess Pea…

ZAP!

The crackle of magic from Tallulah's wand hit Arthur instead.

"**Stop this at once!**" boomed a voice.

A witch with a rippling red cape and the librarian wizard clinging on to her shoulder hurtled down the corridor towards them, followed by young witches and wizards. Princess Pea could only guess this was Madame Merry and her pupils from the Witch Academy.

Tallulah froze. Cedric cowered behind her.

"I'll be taking my wand back, Tallulah Twist!"

Madame Merry plucked the wand from

Tallulah's hand, then landed her broomstick.

Meanwhile, Unipiggle had also decided to take action. He pushed straight past Cedric, through the hole in the pumpkin and into the Queen's bedroom, where he sat his large piggy bottom squarely on top of Super Spells & Extraordinary Enchantments. He wasn't going to take any chances.

"Super job, Unipiggle!" cheered Princess Pea.

"Squeak!" A tiny mouse wearing a wonky little pixie hat scurried up Princess Pea's leg and onto her shoulder.

"Oh, Arthur, thank you! You shielded me from the spell!"

Tallulah was starting to look guilty.

"I was just having a bit of fun, Madame Merry!" she protested meekly.

"Fun?" cried Madame Merry. "You've caused a proper **Witch Emergency** with all the wicked spells you've been casting!"

The little librarian wizard looked stern. "What do you think the King and Queen will do when they find out about your misuse of magic, Ms Twist? I wouldn't

be surprised if they banish you from the kingdom!"

All the other young witches and wizards gasped and Princess Pea nodded. The Queen might forgive a bit of mud and mayhem, but she would not take too kindly to being turned into a unicorn.

Tallulah gulped and turned pale. "Cedric and I only wanted to try out some real magic!" she pleaded. "I ran away because I got bored of non-magical lessons. I'm no good at cauldron cooking or broomstick maintenance. When I saw Princess Pea leave the library yesterday with that spell book, I couldn't resist following her; I was desperate to learn some spells!" Tallulah started sobbing. "I don't want to be banished. I promise I'll never do it again!"

Princess Pea felt a pang of sympathy. Maybe Tallulah wasn't so different from her after all…

The Princess sighed and folded her arms. "As the Royal Princess I can make sure the King and Queen *never* find out what happened today, but you must set to work straight away and help perform the reversal spells. We only have a few hours to change everything back. It has to be done before midnight or all the spells you cast today will be permanent!" she warned.

Tallulah looked astonished. "I didn't read that bit." She sniffed. "I was going to turn them back *eventually*... But, thank you — we'll do anything, won't we, Cedric?"

Cedric folded his wings sulkily and let out a small, resigned honk.

"You can start by taking that crown off, Tallulah!" scolded Madame Merry.

Unipiggle grunted approvingly, picked up the spell book and presented it to Madame Merry, who quickly took charge.

"Wands at the ready, we've got magic to do!"

10
Goodbye, Unicorns

Princess Pea was still feeling nervous because midnight was fast approaching and there was so much to put right in such a short space of time. Everyone had to work together to cast the reversal spells. Firstly, Unipiggle helped Tallulah turn Arthur the mouse back into a pixie, while Madame Merry taught her students their first proper spell: making the librarian wizard full-size again (they managed this perfectly but forgot about his hat).

"Now, Tallulah, you must go and un-enchant the King and Queen immediately, but don't let them see outside until we've performed the reversal spells on everything else," warned Madame Merry.

Princess Pea and Unipiggle followed Tallulah down to the Grand Hall while Madame Merry and the others headed out to the garden to tackle the vicious plants.

Princess Pea closed all the hall curtains and Unipiggle shooed the remaining pixie-frogs out into the night to be un-enchanted by the young witches and wizards.

Tallulah placed the Queen's crown back on the pink unicorn's head and waved Madame Merry's wand. (She'd been allowed to borrow it

again.) Princess Pea couldn't quite hear the spell
Tallulah chanted, but it must have done the job
because…

The unicorns vanished and her parents
reappeared.

Unipiggle sighed with relief. He didn't much
care for unicorns.

The King immediately picked up his ukulele and began to strum… "Ooh, my throat is a little hoarse," he said with a cough.

"Goodness, what has happened to the sofa?" said the Queen, inspecting the damage.

Tallulah, who had forgotten to mend it, distracted her by starting a charming conversation with the royal couple and handed over an official-looking piece of paper. Princess Pea wondered what it was.

Then she and Unipiggle peeked out the window. Even in the dark, the garden looked much less dangerous (and in some places, a little more fun!).

Unipiggle oinked to Tallulah, who bowed to the King and Queen and said goodbye.

On the way out she winked at Princess Pea. "See you again soon!" Then she whistled for Cedric and jumped on her broom to join Madame Merry and the other witches and wizards as they whizzed away into the night sky.

Unipiggle heard a distant clang as the librarian wizard shut the palace gates behind him. He was taking the spell book back to the library to put it in a VERY safe place.

Princess Pea turned and ran over to her parents and gave them a hug. She'd missed them.

"I'm so pleased you've passed your Princess Training with flying colours!" said the Queen, beaming. She handed Princess Pea the piece of paper. It was a certificate!

Tallulah Twist's
Top Princess Training

This is to certify that:

Princess Pea & UniPiggle
have passed their training
with merit. Tallulah CEDRIC

"Ms Twist was full of praise for your princessing and…er…piggy-prancing abilities. So to celebrate we're having a special magic evening tomorrow!" the King said proudly.

"Magic?" asked Princess Pea. "Isn't that banned?"

The Queen smiled. "Tallulah informed me that if I allow magic just for one evening, some highly recommended witchy friends of hers can perform a most magnificent firework display! She promised it would end too. None of that never-ending nonsense like before. And it will be a silent display, of course. Bangs are *most* uncivil. Isn't that a wonderful idea?"

Princess Pea couldn't believe it. Tallulah really could work magic!

The clock in the hall chimed midnight.

"Goodness!" exclaimed Queen Bee. "Is that the time?"

Princess Pea yawned. Unipiggle yawned. It had been a very long adventure.

A Magical Evening

Feeling refreshed after a deep sleep
and a day of *normal* lessons, Princess
Pea and Unipiggle gathered on the
Parade Lawn the next evening with
everyone from the palace. Arthur was
handing out warming mugs of soup made
from the remains of the giant pumpkin.
Up in the sky, the witches and
wizards from the academy tried out
their new magic skills. Unipiggle let

out a thrilled squeal on seeing the
sparks and flashes of the fireworks and
joined in with a few zaps from his horn.

Tallulah Twist landed nearby and
Cedric waved a wing and even managed
a little beaky smile.

"Would you like a go?" Tallulah
offered Princess Pea her broomstick.

"Er…okay! Hop on, Unipiggle!"

Wooooah! Oops!
Wheeeeee!

The King and Queen clapped politely as the firework display came to a spectacular finale.

"Imagine being able to do magic!" mused the King, munching on a carrot.

"Yes, imagine that!" Princess Pea smiled, still dizzy after her exhilarating broomstick ride. She tickled Unipiggle behind the ear, and admired his new purple trotters. No one needed to know she'd memorized a colour-changing spell.

They'd had a fabulous magical adventure together and now they wouldn't forget it!

HOW TO DRAW A UNICORN

You will need: a pencil, a black pen, a rubber and
colouring pencils.

Step 1: Use a pencil to draw...

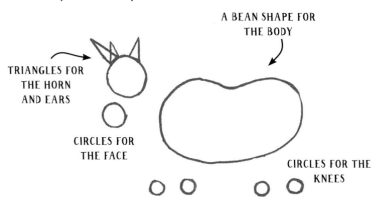

A BEAN SHAPE FOR
THE BODY

TRIANGLES FOR
THE HORN
AND EARS

CIRCLES FOR
THE FACE

CIRCLES FOR THE
KNEES

Step 2: Connect the shapes with straight lines.

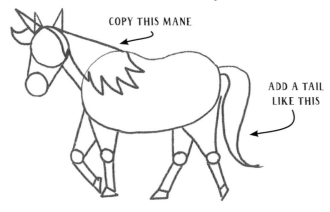

COPY THIS MANE

ADD A TAIL
LIKE THIS

Step 3: Use a pen to draw your unicorn on top of the pencil shapes.

ADD EYES AND
NOSTRILS

Step 4: Wait for the ink to dry, then rub out all of the pencil lines. Now it's time to colour in your unicorn, using the colouring pencils!

WHAT SPECIAL EXTRAS
DOES YOUR UNICORN
HAVE? A RAINBOW HORN?
A MOUSTACHE?

WHO WOULD YOUR ROYAL COMPANION BE?

Princess Pea has an unusual Royal Companion — Unipiggle the Unicorn Pig! Use the lists below to reveal the perfect combination for your very own Royal Companion.

Find the month of your birthday:

January	Dancing
February	Mermaid
March	Chocolatey
April	Witchy
May	Rainbow
June	Unicorn
July	Sparkly
August	Fire-breathing
September	Fairy
October	Piggy
November	Enchanted
December	Jumping

Find the first letter of your name:

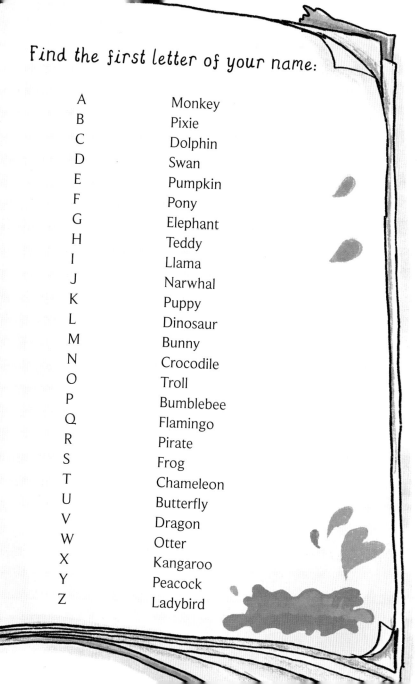

A	Monkey
B	Pixie
C	Dolphin
D	Swan
E	Pumpkin
F	Pony
G	Elephant
H	Teddy
I	Llama
J	Narwhal
K	Puppy
L	Dinosaur
M	Bunny
N	Crocodile
O	Troll
P	Bumblebee
Q	Flamingo
R	Pirate
S	Frog
T	Chameleon
U	Butterfly
V	Dragon
W	Otter
X	Kangaroo
Y	Peacock
Z	Ladybird

HANNAH SHAW

Hannah Shaw *is a multi-award-winning author and illustrator. When she was little she wanted to be a gymnast or a champion rollerskater or a penguin keeper but instead she picked up a pen and began to draw.*

Hannah now lives in Gloucestershire with her messy family. One day she hopes to meet a magical pig, but until then, she's very happy bringing UNIPIGGLE to life with her words and pictures.

Find out more about Hannah Shaw at
www.hannahshawillustrator.co.uk